The Town that Fooled the British

A War of 1812 Story

By LISA PAPP and Illustrated by ROBERT PAPP

Sometimes it doesn't take a giant to defeat one . . .

Click, clack, clack. The August air broke with the sound of shoes running wildly along the docks. Henry Middle's feet carried him fast, skidding around corners, kicking up the smooth Maryland dirt.

No, the day would not stay quiet.

"The British have captured the river!" Henry cried through the door of his father's shop.

That's the way the news came. It was summer 1813 and the people of St. Michaels' worst fears were coming true—a British attack.

Tucked along the banks of the Chesapeake Bay, this tiny river town had been well hidden.

But now the British saw St. Michaels as a threat.

St. Michaels was a town of shipbuilders. Eager and well-skilled, her citizens crafted some of the most valiant ships on the sea. It was their own Baltimore Clippers and other powerful schooners that struck fear in the mighty British Navy.

Weary of their losses at sea, even the British newspapers were calling for destruction of the American towns that made the *great warships*.

St. Michaels could no longer hide from the war.

For weeks, the British had been snaking their way up the Chesapeake Bay, harassing villages and burning towns. And now it was clear they had chosen their next target.

Henry struggled to catch his breath. "I saw the scouts riding in. I overheard what they said! Is it true—are the British really coming?"

Even before his father could answer, Henry saw gunpowder and a musket on the table. Henry's father served in the town's militia.

"I fear it is true," he said, pulling on his uniform jacket. A loose button spun to the floor and Henry picked it up.

"What can I do?" Henry said, slipping the button into his pocket.

"Not now, my son. There will be meetings, so I must hurry." Still wanting to help, Henry reached for his father's canteen. But his father spoke first. "Evacuations will begin soon, Henry. I want you home with your mother and sister."

"But I . . ." Henry began, then seeing his father's face, said no more. Henry stepped out of the shop, wishing he could do more.

The news spread quickly through town. When Henry arrived home, his mother and sister were already in the garden. "We'll harvest what we can," his mother said, "for when they come, we may lose everything."

Henry imagined British soldiers foraging through their garden, taking what they pleased. He refused to think about what could happen to his house and to the room he had always shared with his sister. Beneath the darkening skies, some of Henry's fear was replaced with anger.

Henry's mother folded the last of her herbs into a linen cloth while his sister clung to her doll. "We'll not be joining the evacuation," she said. Henry's mother was skilled in nursing and wanted to be available if needed. "Our cellar is well hidden; we'll be safe below."

Henry watched his mother lift two lanterns from the tiny nook beneath the window. "'Tis a shame," she said. "Your father will have greater need for these than we will."

"Let me!" Henry pleaded, still wanting to help. "I can find father–I can bring him the lanterns." Without waiting for an answer, Henry tucked the lanterns beneath his arms and raced for the door.

"Wait!" his mother called.

Henry froze. "I want to do *something*."

His mother placed her hands on his thin shoulders. Then, she looked into his eyes and understood. "Quickly, my child. Make haste!"

Henry dashed into the street and gasped.

The evacuation had begun. Families, carrying what they could, crowded the village streets, driven by a new sense of urgency. Those unable to walk were carried in carts while livestock clamored alongside.

Henry quickened his pace. I have to find father, he thought again and again.

When Henry arrived, St. Mary's Square was swarming with soldiers. Militia marched in lines while scouts raced by on horseback.

Clutching his lanterns, he searched for his father, but in the sea of uniforms everyone looked the same.

Above the bustling square, a strong wind brought heavy clouds and Henry felt the start of rain.

A unit of men hurried past, talking nervously of cannons and ships and British soldiers clad in red. Not a one seemed to know the hour the British would come. Only that they were coming.

"There will be cannons, no doubt, and gunmen coming ashore," said a man Henry had not seen before. "They will be well trained and dangerous." The voice belonged to General Perry Benson, who had fought boldly in the Revolutionary War.

"We are ready to fight," answered a soldier, "but what are men against cannons?"

Henry shuddered; a part of him wished he were home with his mother. Now soaking wet, his tears mixed easily with the falling rain and he almost didn't know he was crying.

Henry clutched the lanterns tightly. One face blended into another. He scanned the crowd again. Where was his father?

Deep within the mist, the British celebrated their luck! For this storm created the perfect cover for their lurking ships. Their time had finally come to destroy the renowned Maryland shipbuilders.

C . . R . . E . . A . . K . . the British ships leaned and felt their way through the clouded Chesapeake waters.

At St. Mary's Square, evening drew close and with it the dread of what was coming. The constant talk of cannons filled the air. Henry's heart raced, beating faster than the pouring rain. With the lanterns pressed tightly against his chest he suddenly remembered his mother's words … *Your father will have greater need for these…*

"The lanterns!" Henry shouted.

Still searching for his father, Henry saw a buttonless sleeve sweep past.

"Father!" Henry said against the rain. "The lanterns–we can hang them in the trees." There was no response. Reaching for his father's arm Henry stumbled and found himself face to face with the general instead.

General Benson leaned forward, the water pouring from the brim of his hat.

"What did you say?"

"The lanterns," Henry said. "We can hang them in the trees."

Henry's father, stirred by his son's voice, pushed his way through the crowd.

"Sorry, sir," Henry's father said. "I didn't know he was here, I'll…"

But the general's eyes remained on Henry.

Slowly he began to smile. "Gather all the lanterns!" he commanded his men.
"Search the town, find every last one."

Into the branches of trees they climbed and onto the masts of ships, upon every high
place, the lanterns were hung.

Throughout the night, the message was sent: douse all the town's remaining lights!

Henry reached for one more lantern but his father shook his head, "Your mother needs you now. Go." Henry nodded; then, taking one last look at the lanterns, raced for home.

And so it was, in the predawn of August 10, 1813, amid heavy fog and driving rain, the British arrived at St. Michaels.

Aboard the British brig, cannons lined the ship. Soldiers stood ready, eager for battle.

"Find your marks! . . . FIRE!"

The cannons roared, one after the other, chasing the lights of the tiny town, thundering across the water.

BOOM . . . boom BOOM! Gunpowder scorched the air. Metal wheels ground against wood as the cannons were packed and reloaded.

The bombardment continued without rest, for the British were well stocked.

The cellar offered little comfort as the deafening sound of cannons splintered the air. Henry rolled the button over and over in his hand. All he could do now was wait.

With each new wave of attack, his stomach churned with uncertainty.

"Are they getting closer?" his sister asked. "Where is Father, is he safe?"

"Shhh, my child," was all his mother would say.

Finally, before the breaking dawn, it ceased. All became still.

As the first bit of sunlight spread across the skies, Henry crept to the door and dared to look out. A broad figure moved toward him. Henry recognized the familiar walk and at last his father's face came into view. He held a broken lantern in one hand.

"Father!" Henry cried, running toward him.

Soon he was wrapped in his father's arms. "It worked," his father whispered.

With nothing to aim at but the dim lights hung high in the trees, the British overshot the town entirely. St. Michaels was safe; not a single home or ship was lost in the battle. Still cloaked by fog, the British ships skulked away, assuming victory.

Henry's father loosened his grip. "Henry," he said, looking proudly into his son's eyes, "sometimes it doesn't take a giant to defeat one."

Dedicated to the people of St. Michaels, both past and present,
for keeping alive the American spirit.

Lisa and Robert Papp

Text Copyright © 2011 Lisa Papp
Illustration Copyright © 2011 Robert Papp

All rights reserved. No part of this book may be reproduced in
any manner without the express written consent of the publisher,
except in the case of brief excerpts in critical reviews and articles.
All inquiries should be addressed to:

Sleeping Bear Press™

315 E. Eisenhower Parkway, Ste. 200
Ann Arbor, MI 48108
www.sleepingbearpress.com

Sleeping Bear Press is an imprint of Gale,
a part of Cengage Learning.

Printed and bound in the United States.

First Edition

10 9 8 7 6 5 4 3 2 1

Library of Congress Cataloging-in-Publication Data

Papp, Lisa.
The town that fooled the British: a War of 1812 story / written by
Lisa Papp; illustrated by Robert Papp.
p. cm.–(Tales of young Americans)
Summary: On August 10, 1813, with the British navy advancing
up the Chesapeake Bay to destroy the shipyards in St. Michaels,
Maryland, young Henry Middle thinks of a way to save his home
town from British cannons.
ISBN 978-1-58536-484-8
1. United States–History–War of 1812–Naval operations–Juvenile
fiction. [1. United States--History–War of 1812–Naval operations–
Fiction. 2. Saint Michaels (Md.)–History–19th century–Fiction.] I.
Papp, Robert, ill. II. Title.
PZ7.P2116Tow 2011
[E]–dc22
2010032867

Printed by Bang Printing, Brainerd, MN, 1st Ptg., 03/2011

Author's Note

Today, St. Michaels is a gently bustling tourist town. The
streets are laid out exactly as they were in 1813, and if you walk
the narrow lanes by the harbor, you can imagine what life was
like for a small boy during a time when America was learning
that becoming a nation held its own growing pains.

Although Henry Middle is a fictional character, the events
surrounding the defense of his town are real. General Perry
Benson, who fought with George Washington in the War for
Independence just 30 years prior, played a key role in defending
the town.

In telling this small part of a larger story, I hope to spark an
interest in a much-overlooked part of our country's heroic
beginnings. This was a war that gave birth to our "Star Spangled
Banner," the icon Uncle Sam and, many believe, gave the White
House its popular name. Just as my own interest was sparked
when I discovered my ancestors, the Fighting Meekers, fought
in the Revolutionary War and even met George Washington, I
hope this story will encourage you to explore a bit of your own
history and to discover something new about your country.

Many thanks to all the re-enactors who give their time and
finances so that we may enjoy and learn firsthand about our
great country's history. A special thank you to our friends from
The Baltimore United Volunteers, 4th Company, 5th Regiment
for their generous time and wonderful acting skills. Loads of
gratitude to Mystic Seaport, Connecticut, and, of course, the town
of St. Michaels, Maryland, for all their help and enthusiasm and
for preserving so beautifully a piece of our history.